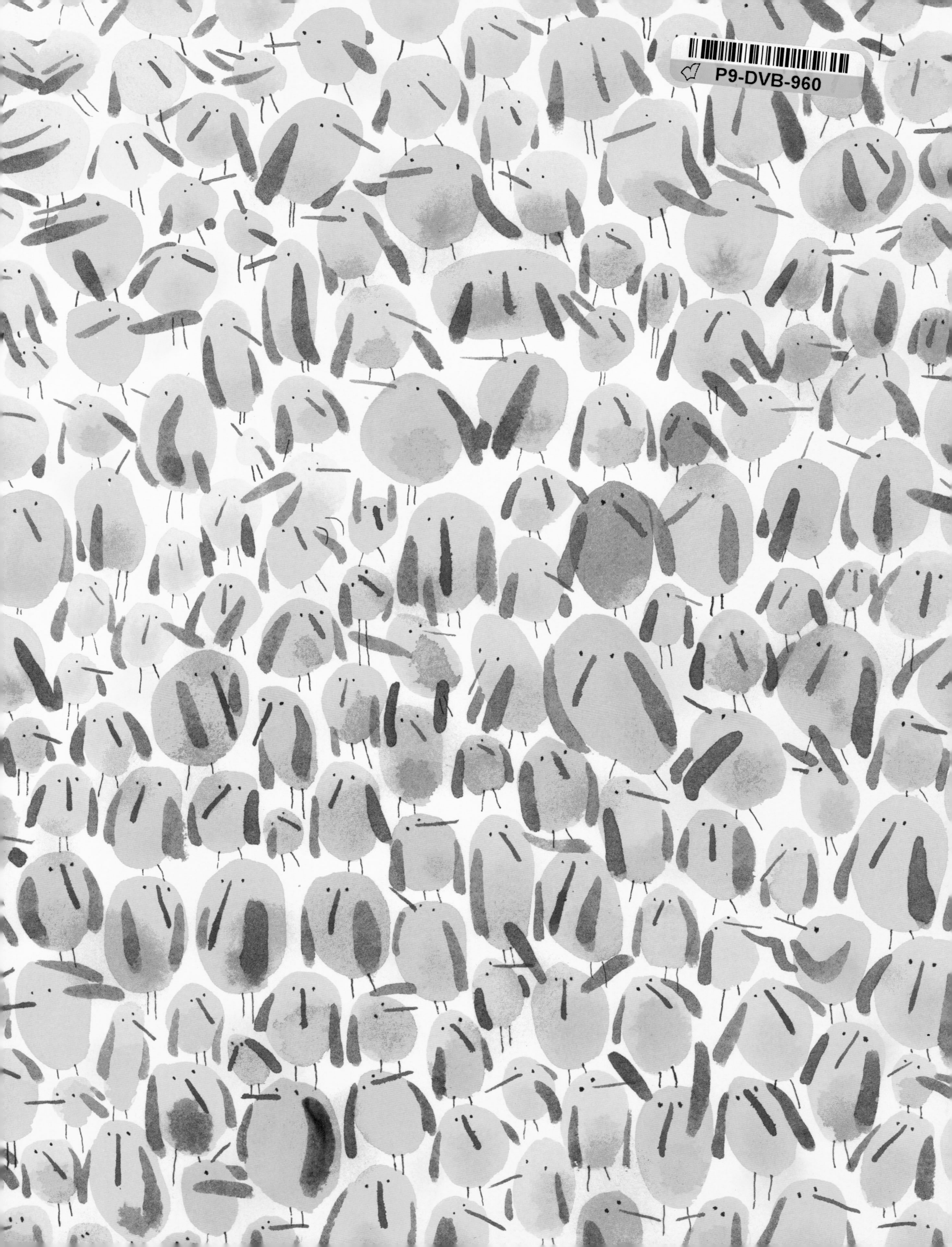

First published 2021 by order of the Tate Trustees
by Tate Publishing, a division of Tate Enterprises Ltd,
Millbank, London SW1P 4RG www.tate.org.uk/publishing

A catalogue record for this book is available from the British Library

ISBN 978 1 84976 761 3

Distributed in the United States and Canada by ABRAMS, New York
Library of Congress Control Number applied for

Printed and bound in China by C&C Offset Printing Co., Ltd

The Fantastic Flying Competition

Tjibbe Veldkamp
& Sebastiaan
Van Doninck

Translated from Dutch
by Kristen Gehrman

Welcome to The Fantastic Flying Competition for birds!
All the teams are ready to go — all except one, that is . . .
Where are the owls? Team Owl is late!
Did those night birds oversleep *again* this year?
The countdown begins:

three . . .
two . . .
one . . .

And off they go!
No, wait, not everyone — Team Flamingo is stuck.

**Those pink birds
can't get off the ground!**

What's going on down there?
Team Hawk takes the lead.
Those hawks are as fast as ever . . .

... and what's this? The hawks are aborting their mission!
Looks like somebody hit the ejection button, but why?
What a sensation, and so early in the race!
Team Ostrich-Penguin is now in the lead ...

After an excellent breeding season,
Team Ostrich-Penguin — huh?
What's that I hear?

PFFFFFFFF...

There's a hole in their hot air balloon!
Hopefully they've got parachutes on board . . .
Phew! That's a relief.
Team Woodpecker is now in first place . . .

. . . but are they losing speed?
They most certainly are!
Team Woodpecker has **completely** stopped!

That's bad news for those birds.
Their propeller is ruined!
And the chickens have just passed them.

Team Chicken takes the lead,
but look who's just a beak's length behind — Team Bat . . .

. . . the reigning Upside-Down-Flying Champions.
Wait, what's going on over there?
It looks like Team Bat has hit . . . **a cloud?**

That's strange!
That's just bizarre!
What kind of crazy
cloud is that?

Only four teams left in the race . . .

. . . no, make that **three** teams left in the race —
Team Toucan is losing fuel!
They've sprung a leak! Those toucans are toast!
These birds sure are having bad luck this year!
Seven teams are already out . . .

. . . and are we about to lose an eighth?

Team Hummingbird has lost control!

Team Hummingbird is headed off course!
Where did this snowstorm come from?

It's down to
Team Chicken
and Team Pelican . . .

. . . and looks like the pelicans have abandoned ship!
This is wild! The pelicans have flown the coop,

right before the finish line!

Team Chicken is the only team left . . .
and it looks like they're already celebrating.
They're going to win this wacky race,
that's for sure . . .

But wait, what's this?
I see Team Ostrich-Penguin and the flamingos,
the bats, hawks, woodpeckers and toucans,
the hummingbirds . . .
and here come the pelicans too!

What are they up to?

Are they coming to cheer the chickens on?

Uh-oh! Oh no!
The birds are trying to
stop Team Chicken!
They can't do that!
Those birds are cheating!

Team Chicken crashes to the ground!
We've never seen anything like it—
all the teams are out of the race!
Looks like there'll be **no** winner this year!

But hold on a second . . .
Who's that drifting over?
Could it be those sleepy birds
made it to the race after all?

FINISH

The jury has reached a decision.
Team Chicken gets disqualified —
but what did they do wrong?
And the trophy goes to . . .
Who would have thought!
Last year's losers . . .

Team Owl wins the

Fantastic Flying Competition

for birds!

(Want to see the race again? Flip back to start for an instant replay . . .)